WARNING

This book contains sexually explicit scenes and adult language. It may be considered offensive to some readers. This book is for sale to adults ONLY.

* * * * * * * * * * * * * * * *

Please store your files wisely where they cannot be accessed by underage readers.

DISCLAIMER

ISBN-13: 978-1988083063
ISBN-10: 1988083060

Other Books by Carla Coxwell:

<u>Torrid Exposure New Adult Romance Series</u>

April is finished with school and ready to build a career. Coming from a well-to-do family, she has decided to reboot her life completely. With family scars too deep to mend, April craves a fresh start. But the past is harder to shake than April ever would have imagined. At the center of it all is Bennett, an old family friend who is the heir to a billionaire media mogul company. Bennett and April haven't been able to stand each other since they were kids. But as the world shifts, the two of them discover the past might be the key to their future.

<u>Devil's Advocate BBW MC New Adult Romance Series</u>

When Kristie comes home from college, the last thing she is expecting is her world to be turned upside down by the appearance of her step-brother, Gray. Gray is rash, impulsive and breaks the law. Kristie's mom asks if she can try to befriend Gray, in hopes to get him on the straight and narrow. The plan backfires, however, as Kristie finds herself falling for Gray. Is it possible he feels the same way? The connection between them threatens to tear down everything Kristie has ever held dear.

<u>Fifty Recipes For Disaster New Adult Romance Series</u>

Trying to win a competition for best chef is cut-throat business. Kiara Sands has just won the opportunity of a lifetime. When she arrives at Fission, she has no idea just how much her life is going to change. She's immediately introduced to Jenny Foster and Robbs Martin, her competitors in the cut throat competition. The only thing Kiara finds more distracting than Robbs' hateful attitude is the handsome executive chef, Paul Weston. It doesn't help matters that Paul is quite taken by Kiara, and showers her with more attention than he gives her competitors.

<u>Star Bright New Adult Romance Series</u>

Torn between her feelings for her agent, Jon, and Rich, a charming bad boy who has ties in the movie industry, Jenny finds herself working through her own past to try to get a grip on her present. As she struggles to learn the lesson that in Hollywood not everyone is what they appear to be, Jenny tries to become a person that she can be proud of. Will she be able to find love and success in Hollywood? Or will she be dragged down by her past forever?

Get the latest update on new releases from the author at:

https://www.carlacoxwell.com/newsletter

This book is Part Two of the "<u>Obsessed Bounty Hunter Romance Series</u>"

1 - Secrets Revealed

Jacqui Schneider couldn't help it. Every time the memories of her family's brutal murder haunted her, she had to escape. The only thing that could replace her sorrow was sex... and lots of it. And so Jacqui developed a pattern of self-destruction by sleeping with random men that she picked up at a local hotel bar. One day, Uncle Max, an old family friend, appeared. He revealed a secret about her father that would change her life forever.

2 - Heart Surrendered

Jaqui thought the training was tough. But keeping her mind concentrated on her task was even tougher after meeting her new trainer. Adam had a rugged handsome face and ripped abs. She hated that Adam was so demanding. Jacqui's boxing technique was never up to his standards. How can she hate someone so much and yet feel such strong attraction? Was he flirting with her while trying to show her the correct stance? If so, the game of seduction was on.

3 - Rapid Pulse Bounty

With her new skills fully developed, Jacqui was a confident bounty hunter with a few successful captures under her belt. Things were looking up for her. The only thing missing in her life right now was Adam. She hadn't seen him since before her first successful mission. He had left before she could show off her triumph. Jacqui admitted to herself that she was in love with a man who belonged to someone else.

Obsessed Bounty Hunter Romance Series

Heart Surrendered

Book Two

By Carla Coxwell

Copyright Revelry Publishing 2015

Table of Contents

Chapter One

JACQUI CHUGGED the water from the container like a thirsty beast. She just couldn't get enough of it. 'Water never tasted so good, better than an orgasm,' Jacqui thought, as she splashed some straight into her face. Jacqui was parched, grimy, and her body ached like she just went through a meat grinder. She was up at 0400 hours in her jogging suit and trainers. Uncle Max met her at the door of a building that resembled a huge hangar.

When Uncle Max said yesterday that training started today before the crack of dawn, Jacqui thought he meant some light exercises that would involve sit-ups and jumping jacks. She was never further from the truth. The next couple of hours had been the most intensive Jacqui ever subjected her body to. And she knew this was just the start.

Uncle Max led her through a routine of squats and crunches, lunges and hamstring curls until her ass had no more feeling left in them. "C'mon Jacqui, move that body," Uncle Max shouted like a drill sergeant. Then he moved on to pull ups, sit-ups, bicep curls, and the bench press. Her arms and legs felt disconnected from her body. Her hand was shaking so hard she almost dropped the water bottle she was holding. She was grateful for the fifteen minute break the old man gave her.

"Alright, Jacqui… back to work…" Uncle Max shouted from the sidelines. She wanted to complain but didn't have the courage to. When she arrived yesterday, Uncle Max told her exactly what to expect for the next couple of weeks. He was dead serious as he went through the program with her. If he was trying to discourage her, he almost succeeded. But Jacqui was too proud to say it. She had come this far to become a bounty hunter.

Before she even got settled into the cot that would be hers during her stay, Uncle Max talked to her privately in what he called his 'interrogation room.' It was a small building at the back of the property. The walls were lined with an assortment of maps indicating the different states of the United States. There were yellow pins tacked on certain cities within the map. Jacqui looked around curiously. She noticed the different surveillance gadgets like GPS tracking, high resolution cameras, night vision goggles, an assortment of pens, and spy gear which she was seeing for the first time in her life.

A bank of television sets was stacked near the wall manned by a single individual. Jacqui saw it was streaming live from some part of the country she did not recognize. A huge glass cabinet held an assortment of guns, some she recognized from her dad's own collection.

"Take a seat Jacqui," Uncle Max indicated a wooden table with hardback chairs in a small corner of the room. He did not speak for some time and Jacqui had a strong desire to squirm under his intense gaze.

"Are you sure this is what you want because right now I am here to tell you, it's not going to be an easy life," Uncle Max said. Jacqui nodded her head, indicating she understood. When she came to her decision back home on the night she called Uncle Max, she quit her job the very next day. She told her boss she wanted to do some travelling. Her boss gave her the go-signal. "It's probably what you need right now," he even said.

Jacqui wasn't sure what Uncle Max thought about the whole idea. She hadn't heard from him since she made the call. But a few days later she found an envelope that was left on her porch. There was no forwarding address and it didn't look like it came by mail. Inside was a one-way ticket to Utah and strict instructions what to bring along. Only a small backpack was needed for the clothing list. It became pretty obvious this was not going to be some luxurious holiday.

She was met at the airport by a burly, bald-headed man, wearing dark sunglasses on a stern face. He reminded Jacqui of an ex-marine or military man. He ushered her into a waiting SUV, got behind the wheel, and started the engine.

They left the city behind until all Jacqui could see were tall mountain ranges in the distance. A few miles onward, they turned into a small dirt road and followed a winding path until Jacqui noticed a copse of large evergreen trees where they seemed to be headed. The trees covered a large expanse of land, save for small clearings with structures that resembled warehouses or large barns. They drove past these until they came to a smaller building where she saw Uncle Max waiting by the door. He greeted her warmly, but Jacqui sensed a certain formality in his demeanor.

Looking at him now, sitting behind the table with a grim expression on his face, Jacqui was suddenly filled with an overwhelming insecurity. Did she make the right decision after all? But Jacqui remembered the downward spiral she was on. The sex with random guys. The orgasms she needed to get some sleep so she could stop thinking about the tragic events of her life. And she needed a purpose… to find some meaning in her life. To honor her dad's memory so she would never forget. For her mom who supported him all the way, and for Danny, who was never given the chance to experience what life was all about.

"Yes, Uncle Max. I have never been surer about anything in my life," she declared with a certain degree of conviction. Uncle Max smiled, and for the first time since she arrived, Jacqui felt relieved. She knew whatever lay ahead, Uncle Max wouldn't spare her, wouldn't try to make things easy for her. She knew that.

"Ok then, let's get you started. I am *The Agency*. I will be responsible for your training. You will not question my decisions… you will do as I say. The training will be rigorous because you will meet all kinds of low-life scumbags. A lot of times your life will be in danger. But you will be trained in self-defense and handling weapons until I feel that you are totally capable of protecting yourself out there. Then and only then will I send you out on a mission. Is that clear?" Uncle Max asked. Jacqui nodded her head in agreement.

"Alright, settle in. You will be shown to your room. Tomorrow your training starts. And for the next couple of days you will only remember pain," The old man warned her. He wasn't kidding. After five hours of the most intense exercise routines she had ever done, Jacqui couldn't even remember her name. Her body hurt even in places she didn't know existed. And this was just her first day in boot camp.

Lunch had been sparse, with just some fish and vegetables. She was given an hour to rest inside her room which was composed of a bunk bed and a footlocker for her personal stuff. No TV, no telephone, no computer or laptop. Then she was called back again and told to run around a circuit she didn't even notice earlier in the day. She tried counting in her head the number of times she completed a circuit before fatigue settled in and lost count completely. It took all her will power to put one leg in front of the other. By the time Uncle Max called for a halt, dusk had settled and stars appeared brightly in a cloudless sky.

"Supper will be brought to your room. Tomorrow we do the whole routine again," Uncle Max declared before he left. It wasn't a request. It was an order. Jacqui trudged slowly back to her room. There is no time to dwell on the unfamiliarity and sparse surroundings. The bed was a most welcome sight and calling her name. She groaned in pain as she stretched her arms over her head to remove her workout clothes. Her back was racked with pain as she bent to unlace her trainers.

Jacqui managed to splash some water onto her face before falling face down into the soft covers with only her undies on. Sleep came easy for Jacqui that night. A sleep so deep she hardly noticed the appearance of two figures in her room.

"You think she'll make it?" an older voice inquired. "I don't know Uncle Max. You put her through the wringer today," the other replied. Uncle Max sighed as he looked at the sleeping form of the girl on the bed. "You're hoping maybe she'll give up and just go back home?" the second figure asked curiously.

"Yes… this kind of life isn't for her. She's been through a lot already. But I also can't accept throwing her life away with all those men in strange hotel rooms," Uncle Max replied. "Well… you said the same thing about me too, remember? I didn't turn out too badly," the younger man said. "No, Adam, you are doing very well. The fact is… you will play an important role in this girl's future," Uncle Max replied.

"I can hardly wait…" Adam replied, taking in the full breasts and rounded ass of the sleeping form on the bed. "Just learn to keep that cock of yours inside your pants…" warned the old man, with a hint of indulgence in his voice.

The two figures departed slowly out of the room where Jacqui Schneider slept an exhausted, dreamless sleep.

Chapter Two

For the next couple of days, Jacqui endured the rigors of her routine with Uncle Max. Although her body was taking a brutal beating, Jacqui realized her mind was getting sharper. Because she slept soundlessly every night, she woke up with muscles still hurting from the day before, but her mind was ready to defy all obstacles the old man managed to put in her face. Uncle Max varied the routine so she got a surprise every time. He said she shouldn't get too satisfied over her progress. They still had a lot of ground to cover.

Although she trained alone with the old man, Jacqui realized the place wasn't as empty as she thought. She noticed some activities going on inside the other buildings. Sometimes she would hear voices but they were always too far away for Jacqui to hear clearly. Once she heard a steady stream of gunshots, which made her freeze in the midst of her routine.

Uncle Max saw her reaction and quickly informed her it was coming from the firing range nearby. He never introduced her to anyone and Jacqui never questioned him. She went through her training with much enthusiasm, never once forgetting the reason she was here.

On the morning of her second week, Jacqui jogged to the building, ready for her daily workout. She never arrived earlier than Uncle Max although she always woke up before the crack of dawn. Same as always, Uncle Max was there waiting for her.

"Morning Jacqui… come walk with me …" the old man said turning towards a path behind the building where they trained every day. "Morning Uncle Max," Jacqui replied, surprised by the sudden change in their daily ritual. "I thought it would be good if we changed our routine today…" her mentor informed her.

The path took a circuitous route among the trees until they arrived in front of a smaller structure. Uncle Max opened the door. Jacqui immediately saw a boxing ring in the center of the huge cavernous room. Grey metal lockers lined one wall. A couple of sand-filled punching bags hung from the ceiling. The room was lit with a few bulbs from the ceiling, casting shadows on the bags where the light hit them. The rest of the room was dark.

"Check the lockers," Uncle Max said, "there are some training shorts and boxing shoes that should fit you." Jacquie did as she was told and found a black pair, perfectly her size. Spotting a new pair of shorts and razor back shirt still in its packaging, Jacqui removed her clothes in a nearby cubicle and donned the new pair.

Entering the room once more, Uncle Max handed Jacqui some headgear and punch mitts. "Just that…? No gloves…? Jacqui asks amusedly. She was expecting heavyweight gloves instead of tiny mitts. "I was thinking we'd start slow," Uncle Max replied. "Boxing is not as easy as it seems." "Uncle Max, I'll finally get to kick some ass…" Jacqui answered gleefully.

"Not until you give me five hundred with this jump rope," a voice cut in from the darkness. Jacqui whirled around in the direction where the voice came from. From out of the dark shadows a man emerged. He was tall and wiry, lean muscles packed tightly over his sun burnt skin. He was wearing loose drawstring pants that hung ridiculously low over his hips. He was barefoot. But what attracted Jacqui's attention was his face. He had the face of an angel similar to those old paintings one would see in museums.

Jacqui stared, mesmerized as he approached. Then she noticed the chiseled face, the blue eyes which stared back at her with scorn, the sharp nose and full lips that were curled in a half-smile. Longish brown hair, badly in need of a trim, was tied at the back of the nape although some curls managed to escape and formed a halo across his face.

"I see you finally got here…Jacqui, meet Adam. Adam, Jacqui," the old man said by means of introduction. Jacqui didn't know where her tongue went. It probably retracted to the back of her open mouth. Stunning…beautiful…sexy… were some of the words running through her befuddled brain. And she was starting to feel gauche and foolish for staring…with an open mouth. Like a robot, she held out her hand for a handshake instead.

Adam reached out for her outstretched hand but instead of shaking it, he removed the mitts, making her feel very foolish…again. "You won't need these for now," he said quietly, taking the other mitt as well, and handing her the jump rope. Jacqui stared at the jump rope like she had never seen one before. She was glad for the distraction as it gave her a little time to regain whatever was left of her shattered composure.

"Don't worry," Uncle Max reassured her, "he has that same effect on all women. It'll pass. As soon as they find out he's an asshole." Adam let out a loud laugh. Uncle Max turned to leave, sending Jacqui to a panic. "You're leaving, Uncle Max?" Jacqui asked stupidly. "You're in good hands and I have some work to catch up on," Uncle Max replied before closing the door behind him.

An awkward silence ensued as Jacqui stood with a rope dangling from her fingers. Adam looked at her sardonically with one eyebrow tilted upward and said, "Well…do you intend to stand there the whole day? I have better things to do than just babysit for the old man."

"What is his problem?" Jacqui thought to herself. Adam moved toward the edge of the boxing ring, slumped lazily against a post with arms akimbo, urging her to start. Jacqui grabbed hold of the handles on each end and swung the rope over her head. Her first few tries were unsuccessful, making her stumble awkwardly.

Adam's laughter didn't help in any way. Jacqui felt a growing irritation in her stomach as she tried again. She finally got the rhythm and managed to jump, counting softly as she went along. "You did say five hundred…?" Jacqui asked out loud. Jacqui discovered that jumping and talking out loud wasn't such an easy thing to do and stumbled once again.

"Start over…" Adam ordered her from the sidelines. "What?" Jacqui asked, irritated. She had managed almost half when she stumbled. "Are you deaf? Start over…" Adam mocked from where he sat at the edge of the ring swinging his feet. Jacqui started over again as the irritation in her stomach turned to slow anger. She needed to focus her mind. She can do this. She just needed to take her mind off the sexy stranger slowly turning into a tyrant in her mind.

She wished she had known beforehand she would be doing jump rope. She would have worn a stronger support bra instead of the regular training bra she had on. She knew her breasts were heaving with her heavy breathing and her nipples were straining hard through the thin layer of the razorback shirt. Mercifully she got to five hundred and dropped the ropes to the ground. She had no intention of going over that again today.

Adam handed her the mitts and led her to the sand filled punching bag. "Let's see what those hands can do…" he said in a taunting voice. Jacqui gave a wordless answer in her head, "Stroke your cock till your eyes pop out…" But she packed a wallop that sent the bag flying. "Not bad…" observed Adam, "but your stance needs improvement."

Adam moved behind her and stood so close that Jacqui felt the entire length of his body behind her back. He positioned both hands on each side of her waist to steady her. Then his thighs aligned with the back of both her thighs as his feet pushed her ankles open.

"That's one stance…" he whispered in her ear. "And here's another..." he continued. Jacqui's heart hammered wildly in her chest as she felt his palm cross from her waist to her belly then traveled downwards to the front of her crotch. His fingers brushed her mound before proceeding down the front of her right leg. Then his fingers grasped the inner muscle of her thigh before pulling her whole leg backwards. Jacqui felt his hand directly below her vagina.

Seemingly innocent… yet completely intentional. Jacqui knew it. She knew he was pretending to teach her proper boxing posture and copping a feel. She also knew he was toying with her. A primal emotion flared within her… the desire to be conquered. But simultaneously her rational brain told her he was an asshole with a big ego.

If I raise hell, he'll say I have a malicious mind. And laugh at me. If I don't, he'll enjoy himself immensely thinking I'm helpless to do anything about it, were the thoughts in her mind. Jacqui's decision came swiftly. "Two can play this game," she thought to herself as a wicked grin appeared on her face.

The game of seduction was on. "Ohhh…I get it…this feels good," Jacqui said in a husky voice, suppressing the laughter forming in her throat. She let her ass accidentally grind against the front of Adam's crotch and was instantly rewarded with a surprised gasp. She ground her ass even harder this time adding pressure to the swelling bulge inside Adam's pants.

Then she turned her head sideways towards him, opened her mouth and let her tongue follow the outline of her lips. Adam's eyes followed the path of her tongue as it lubricated the skin of her lips. Take that you asshole… Jacqui's inner goddess proclaimed. "How about my hands, Adam… show me the best way to use them," she said in the breathiest voice she could muster.

She proceeded to grab his hand that was still holding her inner thigh. She led his hand slowly upward, letting him feel the swell of her vagina, her flat stomach, and then brushing it gently against her breast. Her hardened nipples gave her away as they screamed in protest against the barrier that was her bra. Even though it started as a game, Jacqui felt the moisture that was slowly forming in her panties. She was enjoying this immensely. Tit for tat. Unfortunately, her body was starting to feel hot.

She had not been with a man since she arrived at boot camp. The fatigue from her daily rigorous routine sucked away all thoughts of fucking for an orgasm. She was doing very well until Adam came along. Heck, he started this. Jacqui tried to ease her conscience. But the feel of a man's hard body against the whole length of her back was just too much to ignore. Plus, Adam smelled of musk and lemongrass soap. A heady combination, given the proximity of their bodies.

Jacqui slumped softly against him, resting the back of her head against his shoulder. Adam's other arm was quick to snake across her waist and pulled her even closer to him until his erection rested between her butt cheeks. From her breasts, Adam's finger followed the contour of her throat, up her chin, and brushed against her lips. Jacqui opened her lips slightly and sucked on the finger before turning slowly around to face him.

"You play hardball," Adam said, his nose inches away from hers, his breath wafting slowly into her face. He was breathing hard and trying to control it. But Jacqui saw how totally aroused he was as his nostrils flared with every breath he took. "You started it," Jacqui answered petulantly, her own breath came in short gasps. "Then let's finish it before the old man returns," Adam answered.

The thought of Uncle Max catching them in the act sent both into a provocative frenzy. He would be mad as hell, but at this point neither of them really cared. Adam bent down and used both hands to hoist her legs upwards. Jacqui straddled him upright, surprised at the ease in which he carried her. Adam shuffled to one of the corner posts of the boxing ring. Using the post to support her back, he pulled at the drawstring on his pants. They fell and gathered around his ankles.

Using his fingers, he clawed at the sheer material of Jacqui's shorts and tugged hard. The material tore away, leaving her with just her panties. Even that did not escape the ferocity of his fingers as he gave it a twist until it too tore apart. He positioned his cock and lowered Jacqui, who moaned with pleasure as the head of his engorged cock entered her slowly. Her wet pussy lubricated his entire shaft. He rammed into her slowly, and then increased the speed as he ground his hips to reach her even deeper. Grunting with every thrust Adam made, Jacqui clung to Adam's neck like a person drowning. She had never been taken this way before. And the feel of his hard shaft rubbing against her clit was like wildfire consuming her entire being. A shudder ran through Adam's body as a huge orgasm overcame him. He pulled out of Jacqui and pushed her against the mat of the ring. Jacqui shimmied backward in a frenzy until her foot touched the edge of the mat. She used this to brace herself.

Adam opened her legs wide and lowered himself until his face was just inches away from her cunt. He knew from Jacqui's quivering body that she was seconds away from her own release. Using his tongue he flicked at her clit repeatedly. Bolts of white heat shot through her entire being. Pressure mounted inside her, leaving Jacqui weak with desire and craving for release. "I'm coming, don't stop…" Jacqui managed to say as a giant wave of indescribable gratification consumed her. Jacqui closed her eyes tightly, mouth forming a silent "O" as the first of multiple orgasms consumed her. She bucked wildly as her body sizzled. Unknowingly, Jacqui clamped her thighs shut as the pleasure was released, inadvertently pinning Adam between her legs.

Adam laughed softly as he rested his head against her tummy. He smelled her aroma and realized he liked it. He could stay between her legs forever. Jacqui opened her eyes after seeing stars explode inside her brain. Her eyes adjusted slowly to her surroundings as blood started to flow normally inside her body. Breathing normally one more, Adam said, "Round one goes to you, Jacqui. You have managed to pin me and we haven't even started on full contact sports yet."

"Yup, remember that next time you try and seduce me again," a languid Jacqui replied as she opened up her thighs to release him.

Jacqui picked herself up from off the floor, ignoring Adam's outstretched hand. She was more concerned about her nakedness than his gallantry after seeing her shredded panties on the floor. "What… are you still mad at me?" Adam asked, surprised at the display of irritation on her face.

"Asshole…" Jacqui muttered, as she picked up her panties off the floor and headed for the bench where she left her training suit. She felt totally embarrassed in her half ass-naked glory while Adam had his drawstrings back on. Adam's guffaws followed her inside the room, adding fuel to the irritation she felt. She was confused and needed to gather her composure. Jacqui had never been in love before. Growing up, she realized she had an appetite for sex. It was one of the reasons she wanted to get her own place back home. After her family was murdered, she discovered that it could make her forget the daily nightmares that tormented her.

But she's been free from those dreams ever since she arrived at boot camp. Why did she fall for Adam's advances? And, honestly… she did entice him too. Jacqui had no answers so she did the next best thing and filed Adam under the category 'Proceed with Caution.'

Chapter Three

"Great workout, Sarah…" Jacqui said, reaching out her hand to pull up a petite, red-haired girl, who was trying to catch her breath on the mat. Anyone seeing Sarah for the first time would think the girl was barely out of her teens. The freckles that dotted her face and the flat chest simply enhanced the impression. Jacqui found out the hard way that Sarah was badass and can kick her butt even if she barely reached Jacqui's shoulder.

It was Adam who chose the girl as Jacqui's sparring partner in their workouts. This was the first time Jacqui managed to pin Sarah to the ground. After weeks of teaching Jacqui the basic moves of boxing, they moved on to different types of martial arts. Adam was an exacting mentor but a good one… Jacqui had to give him that. He made her do the different moves over and over again until she got them perfectly. Jacqui learned to do the ax kick, foot stomp, superman punch, flying knee, guillotine and rear naked choke.

But to Jacqui's consternation, Adam had only demonstrated these moves to her. Since that day in the boxing ring when they fucked each other like two dogs in heat, Adam had never tried to touch her again. Initially, Jacqui regarded this as a sign of her victory. But as the days passed, her self-righteousness slowly turned to disappointment... one she tried to mask by excelling in everything he taught her. But Adam simply regarded her as his student now and had chosen Sarah to be Jacqui's sparring partner.

During her second week at boot camp, Uncle Max finally introduced her to the rest of the group. Aside from Sarah and Adam, there was Eli, the stern faced, ex-military man who met her at the airport. He was in charge with the high-powered weapons. He was visibly impressed with the successive bull's eyes Jacqui scored in target shooting. Jacqui shrugged it off as a recessive gene she probably got from her dad. And then there was Johnny 'The Eye' Rodriguez, a whiz kid who interpreted data streaming live inside Uncle Max's office.

The rest of the motley crew was made up of men and women from different backgrounds, all with different reasons for why they ended up as bounty hunters. Jacqui had developed an easy camaraderie with everyone, except for Adam. She was quite unsure about her feelings for him. But Jacqui couldn't deny the frustration she was slowly building inside her mind. Why was he so indifferent to her?

She had seen how he was with the other girls. And with Sarah he was always sweet, often giving her a hug after a particularly heavy workout. Jacqui had to content herself with high fives as a sign of his approval. But there were no hugs. Shit…not even a pat in the back, Jacqui thought after she kicked Sarah's ass tonight. Adam signaled the end of practice.

"See you in the mess hall," Adam said casually, turning towards the door. Sarah followed right after giving Jacqui a pat on the back.

Jacqui entered the cubicle to change, her thoughts about Adam's lack of interest still swirling in her mind. "Maybe I should have been sweeter to him that night, instead of playing it cool." She thought back to that particular heavy encounter they had weeks ago. "Yes, that's what I'll do. I'll show him I can be sweet, let him know that I am interested." Jacqui made up her mind.

She switched off all the lights in the room and, opened the door and walked slowly towards the mess hall. As she turned a corner, she was taken aback as she saw the outline of two people locked in a tight embrace within the shadow of the building. She stepped back not wanting to intrude and heard a voice speak out.

"It's alright Sarah, things will work out…" It was Adam's voice that Jacqui overheard. Jacqui's heart stopped for a moment, anxious that she may have been seen. And then as realization set in, anxiety turned into heavy disappointment and regret. So, Sarah and Adam… Jacqui thought, before stepping silently back and fleeing towards the opposite direction.

She went directly into her room and flung herself on the bed.

Confusion over what she had witnessed overwhelmed her. She just couldn't understand why her heart felt like it had been sliced in two. It's not like he means anything to me. We just fucked each other. End of story… Jacqui consoled herself but she was not really feeling any better about it. Deep in her heart she hoped they could take their relationship onto the next level. But now it seemed that wasn't possible. Adam was with Sarah now.

Unwanted tears formed in her eyes. She was startled by a loud rapping on her door as she hastily wiped the tears away. "Jacqui…dinner is ready; we're all waiting for you at the mess hall…" Jacqui recognized the voice of Uncle Max. "Err…Uncle Max, is it alright if I pass on dinner tonight? I have a really bad headache and just want to rest…" Jacqui replied, trying to hide the tears from her voice.

"Of course… rest then… Jacqui, is everything ok? You sound really strange," Uncle Max reacted from outside her door. "Yes…yes… it's nothing, Uncle Max…just need to rest…"Jacqui countered back at him. "Alright then…Jac, I need to talk to you later after we eat. Do you think you can make it to my office around 2100 hours? It's important," the old man said. "Of course…I'll be there," Jacqui replied.

Jacqui took a long shower hoping to wash away her depression. A calm resolution washed over her as the water splashed her clean. I'll forget all about Adam and just focus on what I need to do. Fuck him. I hope he and Sarah have a great fucking time together, Jacqui thought although it left a bitter taste in her mouth.

An hour later, a composed Jacqui walked into the office of the old man. She was dressed in a white floral blouse over a pair of denim shorts and white sneakers. Jacqui was surprised to see they were not alone. She thought that this meeting was strictly between her and Uncle Max. But Adam sat in a dark corner of the room with arms crossed over his chest. He had a dark look on his face, seemingly irritated over something.

Jacqui had a suspicion she was the reason. They both stopped talking abruptly when she entered the room. "Ahh… Jacqui," Uncle Max greeted her, "glad to see you're feeling better." Jacqui remained silent; her eyes avoided the direction where Adam sat in the shadows. Uncle Max ushered her to the same hardback chair where he conducted her first interview the day she arrived. He positioned himself on the opposite side of the desk facing Jacqui. He inhaled a long breath and said, "I think you're ready for your first assignment."

Jacqui was stunned over this announcement. She had been looking forward to this day. She often wondered how much longer she needed to train before she would be allowed to go out and track someone. She had immersed herself on the laws of bail investigations. She was ready to kick some ass. "Really Uncle Max," Jacqui couldn't hide the elation in her voice. Uncle Max pulled out a brown manila envelope and handed it to her. "This just came in. I pulled everything I could about this guy from our sources. Take a look at it tonight. If you think you're ready, then you can start tracking tomorrow by daylight," Uncle Max said.

Jacqui eagerly grabbed at the folder but the old man held back. Jacqui looked at him with a questioning look. "Do you think you're ready, Jacqui?" Uncle Max asked with a hint of skepticism in his voice. "Because Adam here thinks otherwise." "I'm ready," Jacqui answered with a hint of irritation in her voice. And then just as quickly, she added, "I beat Sarah's ass earlier today."

"Sarah has nothing to do with whether you're ready or not," Adam's voice cut coldly as he stood up from the shadows. Jacqui swallowed hard, regretting her outburst. Of course Adam was right. She managed to make it sound petty. Uncle Max had no idea she caught Adam and Sarah in a tight embrace earlier in the evening. And Adam didn't know either.

"No…err, what I mean is…uhhm…I train everyday with Sarah, so I know I can protect myself if the time comes," Jacqui added lamely. "That's what I was telling Adam before you came in. This case is pretty cut and dried. Get information about his whereabouts… report to me as soon as you have established that. Is that clear, Jacqui?" Uncle Max asked her. Jacqui nodded her head in agreement.

"Ok… that's it then. Unless… you have anything else to add, Adam?" Uncle Max said looking at the grim face of the man who was slowly capturing Jacqui's untrained heart. "Nothing from me. I think I'll call it a night," Adam replied before storming out of the room.

Jacqui had an irresistible urge to run after him, to offer her hand in friendship. Her pride could withstand the humbling experience of extending an the olive branch. She was ecstatic over this new development and wanted everything to be A-OK in her world. But why did he have to be so difficult? She didn't want to make a scene in front of the old man… didn't want to give him any idea about her feelings for Adam.

So Jacqui bade her Uncle Max goodnight but not before giving him a tight hug. "Thanks Uncle Max," she whispered as the old man hugged her back. Holding her at arm's length, Uncle Max said softly, "I didn't want to say this in front of Adam…but… no theatrics, Jac. Bounty hunting is dangerous, but rewarding. Play it straight. Spot your man, report, and then get out of there. Is that clear?"

Jacqui spent half the night reading through the dossier from the brown manila folder. She memorized the features of the man that accompanied the information about him. The hours ticked by and Jacqui became aware of a floorboard creaking outside her bedroom. Warily, she stood from the bed and opened her bedroom door. The hallway was empty. But a strong instinct nagged at her that it was Adam. The smell of lemongrass wafted in the air. But what would he be doing outside her room? She went to investigate but found no one in the hallway.

Shaking her head in disgust over her own foolishness, Jacqui re-entered her bedroom once more, sat cross-legged on the bed and ran through the papers one more time. When weariness finally overtook her, she stuffed all the papers back into the manila envelope, pulled the light switch and spread her tired body over the bed. Maybe this is what I need. A couple of days away from him will do me good. Put things in the right perspective…forget his intoxicating smell, forget the way his arms felt around me, forget his tongue on my…

Jacqui finally drifted away into a troubled sleep.

Chapter Four

Jacqui spotted the man as soon as he stepped out of the van. He was trailed by a group of five heavily armed men as suggested by the bulges in the back pockets of their pants. The rest entered the cabin as one man remained outside the door. This was the fourth day that Jacqui had been hot on their trail. She was in a small town fifty miles from Utah. She was exhausted. She had very little sleep since leaving the boot camp four days ago.

She almost had her quarry yesterday. But something tipped them off and they left in a hurry before Jacqui could phone in their whereabouts. She got her tip from a gas station attendant who filled up her tank. Showing him a picture of her prey, she pretended to be an ex-girlfriend.

"The bastard refuses to pay support. He fucking gives me a baby and then disappears… I heard from one of his buddies he's here somewhere. Just can't wait to give him spit for all the trouble he gave me," Jacqui moaned. "Yer can try some of them cottages for rent two miles from here. Me wife works there as a cleanin' woman. Says there are some newcomers. But she's kinda scared of 'em. Seems they're up to no good…y'know what I mean?" the attendant said.

Jacqui nodded her head trying to contain the excitement she felt. She traveled in the direction the attendant pointed out and now she spotted the cottages hidden among the trees. It was a decrepit resort patronized mainly by travelling salesmen, truck drivers, and road travelers who wanted a cheap overnight stay.

Jacqui scouted the area before taking up her position behind some thick bushes surrounding a small clearing. The cottages were all within her sight as well as the road leading up to the resort. After almost five hours of endless waiting, Jacqui caught sight of a black van with heavily tinted windows moving at great speed. It came to a full stop at a cottage farthest from the road.

Jacqui positioned the binoculars and peered through the looking glass. Her quarry was the last to step out of the van. There was no denying he was the very same man in the photograph in Jacqui's hand. Knowing that every second counted, Jacqui pressed the call button on the cell phone that she carried in her pocket.

The call was picked up on the first ring. "I've got them. It's a small resort two miles from a gas station in a small town called Burkesville, fifty miles outside Utah," Jacqui reported. "I got the location, Jacqui," she recognized the voice of Johnny 'The Eyes' Rodriguez.

Then a familiar voice came onto the line, "Do you have a positive ID?" "Yes Uncle Max, it's him," Jacqui answered. "You got 10 minutes to get the hell out of there before all hell breaks loose…" Uncle Max declared, before cutting the line.

Jacqui stealthily crossed the bushes, crouching low over the trees before hitting the road. Then she ran swiftly toward her car that was parked in a steep embankment a few meters away. She gunned her engine before making a U-turn away from the resort. In the distance she heard the chop-chopping of a helicopter and met a coterie of police cars with flashing red, white, and blue lights headed towards the direction of the resort.

Jacqui knew she had caught her prey. Her first assignment was a success. A feeling of accomplishment and purpose engulfed her. She wanted to laugh out loud in triumph. She had made her first bounty without endangering herself. She was euphoric and was floating on air. And more than Uncle Max, she had an overwhelming desire to share her success with Adam. He had never left her thoughts throughout the four days that she had been away from him. Who gave a shit if he was with Sarah? She could be friends with him. That was as good a start as any she could think of.

Maybe what he had with Sarah wasn't so serious, Jacqui hoped. She could show him she wasn't a bitch. Yes…they could be friends …for now. These thoughts gave Jacqui the second wind she needed to drive all the way back to boot camp. She didn't make any pit stops… not to eat or relieve herself… driven by some primal call to be with Adam.

She only slowed down when she made a turn on the small dirt road that would lead her through the copse of evergreens to the structures that were hidden beneath the trees. Uncle Max came out to greet her as soon as she stepped of the car. He placed his arms around her shoulder, squeezed tightly, and said, "Well done, Jac. They're all in custody. You've earned your first bounty reward."

A round of cheers and claps met her as she entered the office. Everyone she knew were drinking champagne from paper cups, celebrating her victory. It was an immensely great feeling. Jacqui's eyes swept the room, searching for that one face that had been in the forefront of her psyche. Maybe he hadn't heard about the news yet. Maybe he was on his way to join them? Maybe this time he could at least give her a hug?

"Where's Adam," she asked Uncle Max over the din of the revelry around her. "Adam? Oh…he left a few days ago with Sarah. Said it was something personal. You know Adam. He's full of mystery," Uncle Max informed her. Jacqui felt her world crash and burn all around her. Adam was gone. And he was with Sarah. She thanked everyone, gave an excuse about being beat, and made a hasty retreat to her room.

There was no denying the hot tears as they fell uninvited from her face. There was no denying the crushing pain that wrapped around her heart like a steel band. And most of all, there was no denying the simple truth… she was in love with Adam.

-To be continued in Book 3-

If you enjoyed this title, I would appreciate your leaving a review of the book. Good reviews encourage an author to write as well as help books to sell. Good reviews can be just a few short sentences describing what you liked about the book without having a spoiler. If you could spend 30 seconds writing a review, I would appreciate it: you can review this title right now at your favorite retailer.

Here is a preview of the **next story** you may enjoy:

Rapid Pulse Bounty - Obsessed Bounty Hunter Romance Series, Book 3

JACQUI SCHNEIDER gazed at her naked reflection in the mirror and liked what she saw. She had always been curvaceous since her breasts started to form when she was sixteen years old. She got that from her mom. But unlike her mom, whose modest virtues bordered on obsessive, Jacqui loved to flaunt her sexiness even as a teenage girl.

But since hooking up with Uncle Max at *The Agency*, the daily rigors of the exercise routines the old man made her go through every day certainly have managed to give her muscles the tone that wasn't there before.

Her shoulders seemed broader, giving the illusion of a smaller waistline that curved down to her hips. Her round ass was perky as she gave it a playful smack. Her toned arms and legs gave her body the overall impression of a well-oiled machine. Sweating profusely after a five mile run, her sunburned milky-white skin had a pinkish tinge.

After her first assignment went better than expected, Jacqui gained a certain confidence that she never felt before. The next three captures were just as successful. Everything was going well for her. The changes she saw in her body were merely icing on the cake.

Every successful capture meant more money in her pocket. It would never replace the loneliness she felt in being alone without mom, dad, and Danny, but it was a good start. Jacqui mulled over in her mind how to spend some of it. Travel, perhaps? But that decision was a long way off from today.

The thought that she would never have to worry about money in the future gave her a sense of security she lost when her whole family was murdered. The easy fifty thousand dollars that she earned from four bounty works had been deposited in the bank, together with the money her dad left her.

"Not bad…" Jacqui whispered in approval over her finances as well as the reflection staring back at her.

Picking up the heap of dirty clothes from the floor and grabbing a robe along the way, Jacqui entered the bathroom of her new apartment.

Uncle Max helped her settle into her new digs. He insisted that Jacqui come down to the headquarters every day and keep up with her training. So Jacqui opted for a modest townhouse in a quiet neighborhood five miles away. It was a two bedroom affair, furnished, thus sparing her the tedious task of shopping for her own furniture. The living room and kitchen were roomy enough to keep her comfortable during the times she was home.

The only indulgence she added was a shower stall with overhead rainfall shower, a handheld shower hose and 6 body jets. Plus the whirlpool bathtub that Uncle Max declared was a waste of good money.

Jacqui insisted that taking long showers was an indulgence and won the argument.

This was where she retreated after grueling days of tracking her prey, oftentimes foregoing the luxury of a plain shower when she was on the road.

Jacqui adjusted the knobs of the whirlpool and watched as the water churned gently against the edges of the tub. She lighted a few incense candles and poured lavender bath oil into the water.

She stepped gingerly into the warm water and slithered her whole body against the tub. She closed her eyes and sighed in bliss, basking in the floating sensation, making her feel weightless. She allowed her mind to roam, setting free all thoughts and stresses that accompanied her job.

But it was also during times like these that thoughts she had buried deep in the recesses of her psyche often crept out of their screened-off area where she had buried them.

Like Adam…

She hadn't seen or heard from him since that day she made her first successful bounty. The revelry that accompanied her return wasn't enough to cover up the intense disappointment she felt when she was told he left with Sarah. She cried herself to sleep that night, after admitting to herself the true status of her heart. She had fallen in love with him… fallen in love with a man who belonged to someone else.

Often, she cursed the day they met. Cursed the seduction he laid out for her. She blamed herself for trying to defeat him in his own game which ended with them having sex on the boxing ring floor. His intoxicating scent, the smell of his breath, the steely feel of his arms around her waist, the powerful thrusts as he entered her astride on his hips.

Jacqui crossed her arms around herself longing for Adam's lean arms. Then she uncrossed them to caress the skin of her throat, shoulders, and belly. They felt velvety and smooth to the touch. Unwittingly, her hands moved to her breasts as she lay immersed in the warm frothy water. She cupped both and let the thumbs and forefingers of each hand play with her nipples. She felt them harden under her ministrations as twinges of sexual pleasure traveled down her groin.

Jacqui enjoyed the feeling of her fingers as they slowly moved down to her cunt. Using two fingers, she opened the lips of her labia and let her clit pop out. The whirlpool massaged her clit gently. It felt really good.

She rubbed her exposed nub and added pressure with her finger. Her back arched as a spike of pleasure signaled her arousal.

Jacqui raised herself up from the tub and sat down against the rim. She opened her legs wide as she straddled two sides of the tub. She knew what she wanted, what she needed badly.

She picked up a bottle of lube and applied some on her fingers. Then she positioned her fingers against her vagina and rubbed her clit gently. The heat started to build within her open legs. As the heat mounted inside her, Jacqui added more and more pressure on her clit until it felt on fire. She knew her orgasm was near. She imagined Adam's lips as they flicked repeatedly on her clit when he had her prone on the mat. As the intense heat flaring between her legs became too much to bear, she gave in to a powerful orgasm, uttering Adam's name over and over again.

If you enjoyed this sample then look for **Rapid Pulse Bounty - Obsessed Bounty Hunter Romance Series, Book 3**.

Here is a preview of **another story** you may also enjoy:

Fifty Recipes For Disaster: A New Adult Romance Series - Book 2

"**HOW LONG** on the spot prawns, Chef Kiara?" Robbs asks me with mock reverence from across the kitchen. Two months have passed since I was awarded the apprentice position at Fission. Paul Weston stayed out of the decision. No one was able to outright accuse him of being biased and giving the job to his girlfriend, but the rumors are swirling. The rumors about how I landed my job are the least of my problems, though. Paul and Jenny's upcoming arrival is what really has everyone talking around here.

Every time I think of that fateful morning at Paul's appointment, I'm overwhelmed with the same sick feeling in the pit of my stomach. When Paul called me out of the hallway that morning, Jenny bawled and apologized over and over again. She even offered to get rid of the baby, but Paul and I were against it. Paul had immediately insisted an abortion wasn't an option. I agreed with him, but I still can't wrap my head around the idea that in roughly six months, my boyfriend will have a child with another woman. This wasn't supposed to happen, and I'm helpless to do anything about it.

When the apprenticeship contest ended, Jenny left Fission. It's easier for me to deal with her now that I don't see her every day. Paul spent a lot of time reassuring me that I'm the woman he loves, but a part of me doesn't trust him. Family is important to Paul… he'll want to be a hands-on type of dad, and being with Jenny would make that possible.

A year ago, I'd have never been in this position. The situation unfolding before me is a perfect example of why I never let anyone through my walls. But there is something about Paul that made me drop my guard. I am in love with him, and if this baby is going to be a part of his life then I guess it'll be a part of mine, too. I just hope Jenny keeps a lid on all of the 'baby mama drama.'

"Chef?" Robbs calls loudly and brings my focus back to the present.

"Prawns will be up in three," I tell him.

Never having to put up with Robbs Martin again was what I'd been most looking forward to at the end of the apprenticeship competition. But two days before the contest was over, Paul's prep cook Ernesto gave his notice. Ernesto and his wife had just given birth, and he'd been offered a better paying job that would allow him more time off with his family. Paul was overwhelmed and had no time or patience to interview for a new hire. Before the results of the competition were announced, he opened the prep cook position for one of the runners up. Jenny had already decided to leave Fission and take some time to decide what she really wants to do. Robbs was awarded the job by default. I'd expected the bitchy attitude he'd had during the contest to carry over into his new job, but so far he's actually been pleasant to work with. He shows up on time, he helps the other chefs once his tasks are finished, and he makes friendly conversation while doing so. I'm enjoying his new work attitude, but I still don't trust him any farther than I can throw him. Robbs already showed me his true colors, and I don't give people second chances... except for Paul, that is.

I pull the prawns from the grill, plate them, and carry them to Robbs' station. He sets them next to the vegetables he's already prepped for tonight's seafood chowder.

"Did you toss the shells and tails into the stock pot?" Robbs asks me, as if I don't know what I'm doing.

"Of course I did," I answer politely. I can't stand the guy, but I'm not going to give him the satisfaction of letting him get to me.

"Thanks, Chef," he says with a fake smile.

I nod at him and return to my station. I'm doing an appetizer special tonight, and I need to get everything prepped. I prefer to do my own knife work, instead of relying on Robbs. *I have plenty of time for prep work. It's kind of hard to be a chef's apprentice when the chef is never here...*

The toll Jenny's pregnancy took on my job was even harder than the toll it was taking on my personal life. Paul is constantly leaving work to go to doctor's appointments or to shop for cribs. Once he left just because Jenny was craving cheese soup from Mamma's Kettle and was too tired to leave her apartment to pick it up. I had a lot of freedom in the kitchen, but I fought for the job to *learn* from Paul, not to cover for him.

I can't let myself drown in frustration. Not when a lot of work needs to be done. I fill three stock pots with water and set them to boil on the stove. To one I add cumin, cinnamon, and chili powder. The second gets saffron and kefir limes, while the third is seasoned with basil and rosemary. The pots begin to boil, so I toss a handful of salt into each, add my rice, and carefully replace the lids. I turn off the burners and turn my attention to my proteins. I'm making a sushi trio inspired by different areas of the world. I want to do a marinated beef tartar for the Latin roll, but I'm still torn between a couple of different fish for the Indian and the Mediterranean. I need to consider our stock of each of the fish, so I set off for the walk-in cooler.

"Chef Kiara?" a voice calls from behind me. I turn and see Megan, one of the hostesses, standing in the kitchen doorway.

"What is it now?" I groan.

If you enjoyed this sample then look for **Fifty Recipes For Disaster: A New Adult Romance Series - Book 2**.

Here is a preview of **another story** you may enjoy:

Romeo Alpha: A BBW Paranormal Shifter Romance - Book 2 by Darla Dunbar

"**I AM** coming, my love." Amanda could hear Romeo, even though he wasn't with her. She realized that they had connected telepathically, just like he said they would, and smiled as she spoke back to him in her mind.

"I know. I am fine." She needed him to believe she was okay; even if she wasn't. She wanted to make sure he was at ease.

"I told you; no matter where you go, I will find you. I will come for you." His voice reached her ears as if he were standing in front of her, talking.

"I am coming to you."

"No, my love. I am here already."

She turned when she heard his voice. Romeo stood before her, in the middle of the field. She hadn't realized how far she had actually run. Her steps quickened the closer she got to him. He gathered her close in his arms and chuckled when she started ripping his clothes from him. He kissed her deeply and pulled her into the circle of his arms.

"We are outside, honey. Anyone could see."

"Come on, aren't you a wolf? Besides, Romeo, don't you think it is time to be ourselves?"

"You make a valid point," he said, in between kisses on her throat.

"Good, then, come on. Let's become one with nature."

He chuckled as he slowly made love to his mate there among the wild flowers and fields.

Amanda knew her work wasn't over. Somewhere out there, her brother was coming up with another plan to take her powers, but for the moment, she wanted nothing more than to feel her mate.

As Romeo slid inside her, she moaned deeply. She didn't need any foreplay or fondling. She just needed him inside her as soon as possible.

He flipped her to her hands and knees and slid inside over and over, speeding up until he was taking her with such force that she lost her balance multiple times. She reveled in it, and met him thrust for thrust, until they both screamed in pleasure.

As they lay in each other's arms afterward, they planned their next step in life and as a couple. They planned their eternity together.

It had been a month since the fiasco of Amanda's kidnapping. Amanda had decided to move into her aunt's estate with Romeo, and they were to be formally married in just two weeks' time. Her powers were growing, and she was grateful for Penelope, who came and helped her to control them. Penelope, Audri and Aurora were like the sisters she had never had, and she found herself becoming very close with them all.

Amanda began to notice that Penelope acted a little strange whenever they came around Elijah, though. Being the quiet one, he often stood aloof when the family was together. He was also the polite one and the one that they all agreed to be the most loyal and family-oriented.

He didn't say much, but his eyes would scan the room for Penelope often. When Penelope also noticed this, her cheeks would turn a light shade of pink. She would often avert her eyes, but Amanda saw the few instances where her eyes would meet his. There was a current of electricity in the air. Amanda could feel the effects of it from across the room. Was that what she and Romeo seemed like to others?

Amanda's brother had disappeared along with Lilith, but Amanda knew that it wasn't over. She could feel her brother breathing down her back. She would catch herself looking around, feeling like someone was watching her. Whether he was close enough to see her or he used his magic, she knew her brother was watching. She had often spoken to Penelope about it, and the other woman had decided to increase the frequency of Amanda's magic lessons because of it.

She guessed the other woman could feel the anxiety building as well. Something was going to happen, and it was going to be big. She knew her brother would have something to do with it, would probably be the whole reason behind whatever chaos would ensue. The only problem was they didn't know what exactly to expect from him. He was sneaky and conniving.

Amanda and Penelope were Radiants; two out of the four most powerful witches in the world. Soon, the news would be out, and the other two Radiants would meet up with them. They were sure of it. Amanda was so excited to meet the Fire Radiant and the Water Radiant.

She was sitting alone on the porch when Penelope made her way over. Penelope was petite and one of the most stunningly beautiful people Amanda had ever seen. She seemed so regal in her posture and movements. But she never seemed to hold herself above others.

Amanda had seen her in the dirt playing marbles with some of the kids just the day before. Her white shirt had been brown by the time she stood up. The funniest part was watching her play the childhood game as her tongue stuck from the corner of her mouth. She had an amazing laugh. Her cheeks had been tinged pink, and her long blond hair had been matted at the ends where it trailed the dirt while she crawled around on her knees.

Penelope had relayed to Amanda the nature of her childhood, or lack thereof. Her father had never allowed Penelope to play with other children, and she often wasn't allowed outside. In the beginning, her mother would sneak her out or she would fight with Penelope's father until he would finally give in and let her go out. Her mother very rarely lost an argument with anyone, including her father. Penelope thought it was in part because he was so scared of her. That was the reason for the poison he'd used to kill her. What a coward.

The servants had told Penelope what happened. They had said her father wanted to take her mother breakfast in bed, and he had them prepare the meal. They figured he must have added the poison on his way up the stairs, because her mother was gone the very next day. Their suspicions about the circumstances grew when he always seemed to be with Penelope's adopted sister, who was just a few years older than herself. She was proved correct when she snuck downstairs in the middle of the night. Lilith leaned over a desk with her father behind her. It was an image that was scalded into Penelope's brain. The worst part was the conversation afterward, where the both of them had clarified their plot to kill her mother.

Two of the servants loyal to her mother were standing in the doorway across from her. One of them had grabbed her and covered her mouth as they took her through a hidden doorway back to her room. They had shushed her and stroked her hair. They had tried reassuring her everything would be okay. They told her that they would help to protect her, and they wouldn't let anything happen to her. That was the last time she ever saw them. A new housekeeper and butler started the very next day. From that point on, she had stayed hidden from everyone, especially her father and Lilith. She knew that her mother had given her powers to her, and she studied on how to use them, but never had the nerve to try anything out.

"Hey, Penelope. What's going on?"

"I came to talk. I wanted to talk to you before, but we needed to be alone."

"Okay." Amanda instantly began to feel worried. What did Penelope not want to say in front of the others?

"Well, you know there are two other Radiants, and we will probably be meeting them anytime now."

"Yes. It is exciting to meet new people, especially ones who will have the same powers as we do."

"Yes, but I don't think you know the full extent of your situation."

"What do you mean?"

"Your power is on the line, Amanda." Penelope looked sad for a moment.

"Well, I mean, I know that. Look, I know I have just recently found out that all of this stuff is even real, and I am just now coming into my full blown powers, but I can learn fast." Would they take her powers from her? Could they do that? She knew black magic could, but would the other Radiants resort to that?

"That is not what I am talking about, Amanda."

"Then what are you talking about?" A chill ran down Amanda's spine. Were there more stories; more secrets?

If you enjoyed this sample then look for **Romeo Alpha: A BBW Paranormal Shifter Romance - Book 2 by Darla Dunbar.**

Other Books by Carla Coxwell

- Torrid Exposure New Adult Romance Series

- Devil's Advocate BBW MC New Adult Romance Series

- Fifty Recipes For Disaster New Adult Romance Series

- Star Bright New Adult Romance Series

Get the latest update on new releases from the author at:

https://www.carlacoxwell.com/newsletter

About the Author - Carla Coxwell

Carla has always been a fan of romance novels. To augment what she made waiting on tables to help her way through college, Carla also did some freelance work in the romance genre.

Now she enjoys living vicariously through her characters in her New Adult Romance books.

Connect with Carla Coxwell

I really appreciate you reading my book! Here are my social media coordinates:

Friend me on Facebook:
https://www.facebook.com/CarlaCoxwell/

Follow me on Twitter: https://twitter.com/carlacoxwell

Check me out on Goodreads:
https://www.goodreads.com/author/show/10691544.Car
la_Coxwell

Subscribe to my newsletter:
https://www.carlacoxwell.com/newsletter/

Visit my website: https://www.carlacoxwell.com/